JUNNU's Adventures
Vol-1

Vurity Sulekha

ALL RIGHTS RESERVED

All rights reserved. No part of this publication may be reproduced, stored in or introduced into a retrieval system, or transmitted, in any form by any means may it be electronically, mechanical, optical, chemical, manual, photocopying, or recording without prior written permission of the Publisher/ Author.

JUNNU's Adventures
Vol-1
of
Vurity Sulekha

Ph: +91 63057 36664
E-mail: **sulekha.vurity@gmail.com**

© Vurity Sulekha

ISBN (Paperback): 978-81-982729-4-2

Published By: Kasturi Vijayam
Published on: May-2025

Print On Demand

Ph:0091-9515054998
www.kasturivijayam.com
Email: Kasturivijayam@gmail.com

Book Available
Amazon (Worldwide), flipkart

Dedication

This novel is dedicated to all the lovely,
innocent, amazing children
on this wonderful earth.

Thank You

I am truly grateful to Kasturivijayam Publishers and their team for their support and effort in publishing this book.

Table of Contents

1. JUNNU'S BENEVOLENCE 1
2. A VICTORIOUS JAUNT 8
3. VOYAGE TO FROSTY-LAND 16
4. BIZZARE BLOSSOM 25
5. DIBLI — DIBLI RETURNS..31
6. JUNNU'S VERDICT 39
7. MAGIC PILLOW 45
8. VANISHED WAND..53
9. ADVENTURES OF JUNNU IN FRUIT LAND- I 61
10. ADVENTURES OF JUNNU IN FRUIT LAND -II ..68

1

JUNNU'S BENEVOLENCE

JUNNU's ADEVENTURES

Hai...

I am JUNNU which means "Pudding" I am here with my German Shepherd dog Steffi and its son Bruno.

I ask you out all to my wonderful JUNNULAND.

***

Now we enter into JUNNU'S WONDERLAND where everything is made of pudding! Snow white, smooth and soft pudding castles, moonlit gardens encircling with pudding flowers amid of these tingling pepper flavors and cardamom"s sweetness a huge grandly decorated pearly pompadour pudding fort is of Junnu"s. This is the northeast corner of her palace, here we can see the pudding glaciers.

Her sofa sets, dining sets, cots are made of cottage pudding. They are also panelled with juicy cherries. She rules her kingdom under the guidance of a great sage Ananda. He offered a magic wand which juggles"

***

One cozy morning, Junnu went out for jogging with her friend Steffi. On the meadows they saw a baby pelican which was limping. Junnu was moved. She had taken its limb on her lap.

"Hi, you are not the resident of my land. Where are you from?"

"Greetings your Highness! I am Pansy from Pelican land. I was on a pleasure trip with my friends. Unfortunately, I slipped and got hurt. But no one took notice of me.. Now I am unable to move. If you give me shelter for a few days, I will be allright and can go back to my Place."

"Certainly. But you require some medication. as your limb is severely injured."

"Yeah, your Highness. It is in dire need of medicine. If you permit, I go and call our physician Harry hare from Heal Island," said Steffi.

"Good idea! You hurry up." Steffi is very

loyal, sharp and meticulous.

Junnu took her magic wand and chanted a mantra three times..

"Jooo…Jooon magic wand…

Juggle and kiss

me."

She taps Steffi"s rear portion with the magic wand.

Within no time Steffi flew into the sky with its

wings stretched into the air. "Greetings! Dr. Harry hare."

"Very good morning, dear. How can I do a favour to you?"

Steffi explained the pelican's problem. Harry called her assistant the Squireey squirrel. Both of them climbed on the back of Steffi.

Then Steffi chanted a mantra

"Bow.. Bow.. Magic wand..

Hue.. hue.. Highness..

Bless me to fly in the air."

They crossed mountains, valleys, rivers, villages, fields and reached JunnuLand. "Greetings! your Highness, where is my client?"

"Here it is Dr. Harry," said Junnu.

After testing the wound Harry told that shallot paste was the medicine which could be available on the other side of the mountain, all of them went there.

Harry grinned after seeing the herb and started digging the soil with a shovel. "G...U...RU....RU...H! don't touch my soil," the voice groaned.

Harry froze with fear, Junnu reprimanded the voice and asked,"Who is that?"

I am Dibli Dibli, the monster. I don't allow anyone to touch the soil, really if you are in dire need of shallots there is only one way to fetch them.

"What's it?" asked Junnu. "Your Magic Wand."

"If you give your magic wand, I will give my land."

Junnu immediately accepted the proposal and said "How can I trust you? This task should be accomplished by mutual exchange of wand and shallots."

Junnu chanted and told the monster to recite the mantra..

Jooo.. Jooon.. magic wand.. Jooo…Jooon.. magic wand..

Juggle and kiss me!!!

As the monster was in a hurry, instead of the words "kiss me" it repeated as "kick me." The magic wand banged the monster and eventually the monster fell down and swooned.

Squireey squirrel packed the shallots and all of them returned to Junnuland.

Dr. Harry made the paste of shallots with turmeric and Squireey applied that paste on the wound of Pansy pelican. After three days the wound healed.

Pansy's parents came to know about the benevolence shown by Junnu and her mates. To show their gratitude they brought a gift, it was a multicoloured flower Didhiya." It never dries, and fades. It will be always fresh with perfumed fragrance and work as an elixir. When anyone suffers from a disease then one has to inhale the scented smell. The ailment will be cured."

Junnu accepted the gift and thanked them.

2
A VICTORIOUS JAUNT

One day Steffi went for shopping with Bruno. It wanted to purchase cloaks for Bruno and itself. While returning it saw a camel on the way. It was with its owner. The children rejoiced with ting-tang sounds of its anklet bells. Bruno wanted to climb on it for a ride. Steffi went to the owner and told about the longing of Bruno.

"Okay you ride on my camel but you must pay rupees ten per head."

"But...but... we have no currency. Instead, I can pay the quantity of pudding you require."

"Junnu! the Pudding! Are you from Junnuland? I heard that it's very delicious with the tempting pepper flavours."

"Yeah, ofcourse. Have it." Steffi offered a bowl of pudding as the charge for the ride.

The man tasted one mouthful of it and enjoyed himself with its yummy taste, in the meantime the camel carried Steffi, Bruno and sprinted towards the Junnuland. By evening, they reached their land.

Steffi asked the camel "Can you go alone from here?" "No, infact I don't want to go to that cheat."

"Cheat! Who? Why?"

"I am Canny. My parents named me as Canny because I am clever but unfortunately I was trapped. I am from Sandilova desert. One day when I was alone near the dates plantation this cheat came there and abducted me by making unconscious. He made me to starve for a week, I have become emaciated and followed him blindly."

Woefully it said, tears rolled on its cheeks, Junnu consoled it and assured that it would be sent to its motherland.

***

It was a nimbus evening. Junnu, her friends and Canny camel were munching the roasted mealies.

Steffi asked Canny camel "Are you happy here?"

"Yeah, why not? I am Extremely delighted.. Eating sweet, creamy, pudding I have put on weight. Haven't you observed? But...."

"What but? Any problem?" Junnu asked eagerly.

A little my excellence. Sometimes I feel to see my parents"

No sooner had the camel said that, than a

melodious song with wonderful lyrics loitered in the air. Canny was alert.

Thrash…Thrash…
Sweeeet heart…
Honeeeey hump…
Canny camel…
I am here…
With orange eyes…
Groping near…
Thrash… Thrash….

"Hey! Thrashy…Thrashy… I am here. Come down to Junnu's land." Vigorously Canny called the singing bird.

Slowly the bird had come down and stood in front of Junnu. It was a sober sandy bird with orange eyes, its beak was very sharp and pointed. After seeing Junnu and the rest it thought Canny was in plight. It had taken its tiny razored long pointed needle.

Canny swiftly moved towards Thrashy.

"No Thrasy, please. These are our friends. Don't spite them. They are very affable. Infact, they saved me from the cheat."

"Oh, I am extremely sorry." Apologised Thrashy

"By the way, this is my family friend, well wisher Thrashy…your excellence. It came in search of me." Canny said.

"Greetings! your Highness. We are so grateful to you, now I leave for my land and inform about Canny so that Canny's parents can come and pick her," said Thrashy.

"Certainly. But first you have some pudding. It's our land's special dish and relax. Then you can leave," said Junnu and ordered Bruno to bring some pudding with raspberries for Thrashy.

After relaxation Thrashy under the leave of Junnu flew towards its land.

***

Canny camel's parents and Thrashy started their journey from Sandilova desert. They boarded on a cacti flight, the seats of which were made of aloevera cushion. Thrashy was guiding them. They were bringing a big bowl of dates touching the brim.

The bowl was a unique one. It never be empty and if anyone emptied, it immediately would be filled with dates. Canny's parents wanted to offer that magic bowl to Junnu as a token of gratitude.

All of a sudden the bowl fell down. They bewildered. In no time the flight landed down.

It was a vast honey island! They searched for the bowl. But their efforts were futile. Eventually a servant came there and threatened them to leave the land immediately or they would be in plight.

Thrashy convinced the servant and told him that they lost their magic bowl. After hearing the servant took them to the king's court. The king ordered his servants to grope for the magic bowl.

The bowl was found in a pond of honey. The honey imbibed into the dates. The king tasted and became greedy to grab it as the magic bowl cannot be emptied. The camel couple told the king the reason for their journey towards Junnuland. In order to implement his cunning plan the king told Thrashy to invite Junnu and friends to his kingdom.

***

The palace and garden were decorated colourfully. The king ushered everyone with a feigning smile. Guests were served a cup of honey with soaked dates, a sandwich and an ice cream. The king was mingling in a scornful way. He was enthralled by seeing flying Steffi and the magic wand. He wanted to grab all. So he offered Junnu in exchange with Steffi the dog, to his Ballsy the bee, which produces honey while it dances.

But Junnu refused the proposal and made the arrangements to leave for her land. Ballsy came to know about the conspiracy of its king. It wanted to retaliate and flee from there. So it encountered Steffi and asked a solution for its problem.

Steffi gave a wonderful idea. Ballsy started humming rejoicely and twirled around its king...

I am Ballsy... Ballsy... Am fancy.... fancy....

Dance...Dance....

Sing...Sing

Happy ... Happy... I make you happy...

The bee sang, danced and the fallout was the king indulged in honey ocean.

"Hey! Ballsy stop the song, stop the dance. I am drowned. Please save me." The king said.

"No, your excellence you are a cheat, you deserve this. Bye..Bye. I am going with these guests." said the bee.

The king drowned in the flood of honey. The land inundated in it. Junnu returned to her land with camel couple, Ballsy the honey bee and Steffi.

The camel couple gifted the magic bowl to Junnu and left for their land with their baby Canny.

03
VOYAGE TO FROSTY-LAND

It was a sunny morning. Steffi was plodding in the garden. Suddenly Steffi beheld an icy block in front of it. A polar bear alight from it. Steffi appalled after seeing the bear suddenly.

"Hello, May I know who you are and from where you have come?" "Certainly, I am Polly, the polar bear."

"Polly, the bear?"

"Are you from polar region?" "Yeah, exactly. And you?"

"I am Steffi. Nice meeting you. This is our land called Junnuland. Here everything is made of pudding. Our ruler is Miss Junnu. I am her loyal friend".

"Oh, wonderful! But…" said Polly.

"But what?" Said Steffi

"So these white blocks are of pudding, not ice blocks?" "Yes, by the way why?" asked Steffi.

"God! I will be ruined. I am in bad need of

ice now. If it is not available, I cannot go back and I will die here itself. As a matter of fact, I guessed that these blocks would be of ice as are of snow-white. I thought to have a pleasure trip to this land."

"My God! How can I help you now? Let"s meet our princess. She could show a way for this." said Steffi and had taken Polly there.

***

After pondering sometime Junnu took her magic wand and chanted

"Joo – Joon magic wand …

Show the way to icy land

To land our guest in native land."

She opened her eyes. The wand slowly moved towards East. Then it bent down.

Junnu said, "There will be an icy land in the east. May be in a valley as it is bending down."

"Oh, but there is an ocean in east. How can a valley be there!" Steffi replied in a suspicious voice.

"But my wand never says a lie. Steffi, you explore in that direction." Said Junnu "Okay your highness". Steffi flew towards east and returned soon.

"Ma"am, you said correctly. Near the creek of the mountain the ocean waters falling down into an alley which is surrounded by icy mountains. But it is protected by an icy monster „Farrago" he does not allow even an iota of foreign matter in its land."

"But it is inevitable for us." Junnu murmured thinking seriously.

Polly was frantic. Junnu said, "Steffi, you take the honey bee Ballsy and offer the honey to the monster. It will be mesmerised by the sweetest nectar and certainly offers us the ice block."

"Your highness, may I escort them ? Because it is high time my ice block melted. If I get some ice there, I can survive" Requested Polly.

"Sure, it's good you can follow them." Said Junnu

"Certainly ma'am. Thank you." Steffi flew by spreading its wings on both sides high up in the sky. Polly sat on the right wing and Ballsy on the left. Junnu chanted the hymn with the magic wand.

***

Steffi landed on the crest of the icy mountain with its friends. The monster roared in a spurt of moment "Yer.r.. r.. who is there! I swallow you.. swallow you." It opened its cave like wide mouth. The curved canines protruded out when the monster roared.

"Sure, your Highness. We came here to be your prey. But before that my friend Ballsy wants to entertain with her talent." Steffi told loyally.

"Talent"...! What talent! I am not a folly. Don"t tell all the cock and bull stories," said the monster.

Scarcely the monster told this when Ballsy started dancing and showered the nectar. Honey fell down on the tongue of the monster.

"Yo...yo...yummy... yummy....sooo... sweet what is this! " monster swung with rejoice."

"Hi... who is this angel?"asked the monster.

"Sire.. I am Ballsy. May I know your name?"

It stopped the dance and ascertained. "Sure, I am „ Farrago".

"...so cute name just like you" said Steffi.

Steffi wanted to take the advantage of Farrago"s love towards Ballsy. It gestured Ballsy to raise the purpose of their arrival.

"Sire, please do a favour for me," said Ballsy.

"Favour.. sure! What"s that? Express your wish! I am at your service,"" said Farrago.

"Thank you sir. This is my friend Polly, came from polar region. Unfortunately its vehicle melted. Now we are in dire need of ice blocks to make the vehicle," said Ballsy.

"Okay, you can take. But on one condition, What can I get in return?" "I offer nectar even for your future".

"I don't want that. I am longing you here in

my land forever."

"God... Forever! Please sire, leave me. I pour an alley of honey for you and I come whenever it is emptied."

"Sorry, I cannot help you," Farrago growled.

"Sire please understand my situation. If you help me, I will fetch the ice fruit for you," said the bear.

"Ice fruit! What's that? Where do we get?" monster asked curiously.

"It will be available in our polar land. If we tap the ice fruit once, we get heaps of ice cream."

"I.... ce.... Cream!" monster screamed in hue.

"Yeah...Yeah... so sweet delicious ice-cream and you can dress it with honey layers," said Steffi and Ballsy in chorus.

"Oh, that"s good. But... er...er... how can I trust you?" Farrago groaned.

"We are honest or else I will be here till my friend Polly arrives," Ballsy assured in hurry. It did not want to loose the chance.

"Okay, now you can take the ice blocks you want," said the monster.

"Ballsy.. you don't stay alone. I too will be here till Polly comes back," said Steffi.

"So very nice. Steffi and Ballsy can be here till Polly comes. But if she won"t come, the very moment I swallow you both," the monster screamed out.

"No sire. I come and keep up my word," replied the polar bear and procured some blocks of ice and made an icy vehicle with the help of Steffi and Ballsy.

While doing that task Steffi whispered in Polly's ear that it needn't bring any ice fruit instead it could go to Junnu, she would give an idea to get rid off the monster and rescue Ballsy and Itself.

Polly nodded its head and set off to Junnuland.

***

Surly Farrago scurried around the ice land. It was apprehensive after seeing weird beautiful lass with a magic wand along with Polly.

"Who... who...!" gasped and yelled the monster.

Steffi understood that Junnu had arrived by watching the countenance of the monster and strolled in hue and said "Sire, this is our ma'am Junnu. The ruler of our Junnuland."

"Oh, marvellous Gorgeous lady! Hearty welcome to our land," said Farrago.

"Ha..ha.. I am the most fortunate creature on the earth," Monster cried with joy.

Junnu grinned "You are the luckiest person in

the world," Junnu said and closed her eyes. She chanted a hymn

"Joo.. Joon.. Magic wand..

Twirl the monster,

Twirl..Twirl…Twirl."

Scarcely had the hymn completed when the magic wand rotated around Farrago and it fastened with a magic tether. The monster plunged in the alley of honey and eventually Farrago choked and collapsed.

4
BIZZARE BLOSSOM

It was spring season. There was greenery everywhere except in JunnuLand.

Languidly Junnu was walking in the palace along with her friend Steffi. Junnu was fascinated by the pretty flowers of nearby ornamental gardens.

"Your highness, if you permit me I will go and fetch some beautiful flowers for you." Steffi said.

"No, Steffi, both of us will go there. I am very much yearning to have the wonderful flowers by plucking them personally."

"Sorry to say mam, it's not advisable to go to that strange place." said Steffi.

"As long as we have this magic wand given by sage Ananda there won"t be any danger." Junnu assured.

Junnu took the magic wand and chanted "Joo...Joon magic wand take us to flower garden."

Steffi spread its wings and flew towards the garden and Junnu alighted the magic wand accompanied.

To their surprise the garden was floating in the clouds.

Then suddenly there was a squall. It hit Junnu and Steffi. They astrayed. Junnu ordered the wand to show their path to homeland but it failed. It whirled in irregular circles. Steffi baffled.

Junnu recollected the sage"s words when she was offered the boon of magic wand he said, "Dear it can guide you on land, in water and also in air. But on one condition it guides to the places where normal life exists. That means the living being should be in single form. If it is the conjoint of two or more than two forms, it will be helpless."

"God! we are in danger zone." Hardly had Junnu understood the situation when both were trapped in a flower field between the sky and the earth. At the centre of that there was a big buttercup. It had elongated eyes, sharp nose and a round mouth. It was so pretty. To their wonder it had soft, long, tender legs and soft hands.

"Hi maam, I am a Florianm."

"Florianm! means?" Junnu exclaimed.

"We are the conjoint of flower and animal. We have flower form from face to waist and limbs like animals. We speak, move, eat, and breathe like animals. Interior region of this cotton cloud is our kingdom. I am „Buky" the buttercup. All the varieties of flowers are present in our land. Please apologize mam. I chanted one of the newly learnt hymns from my master, so you were trapped in that gust, I will be blessed if you visit my land and enjoy yourselves the wonders. My cordial welcome to you and your companions."

Junnu smiled and followed Buky with her friend.

There was an odium decorated with bright colourful florets. One end of it there was roses throne on which the king „Mezereon" sat with the queen, Zephyranth".

"Your highness, this is Ms. Junnu the princess of Junnuland, Steffi, her friend. If you permit they stay here tonight."

"Sure. I am so pleased to see you. Please take your seats and enjoy our court dancers programme."

"Thank you your Highness" said Junnu and all of them sat on their chairs.

Angelica, Celsia, Jasmine were dancing on the dais. Turquoise light shaded them. Melodious music hovered the surroundings

***

Junnu was mesmerised with the dance performance and chanted the mantra.

"Joo..magic wand

Joo.. Joo.. magic wand

revere our host with our land's special delicious flavoured pudding."

A heap of cream coloured pudding was ready in a vast utensil. Steffi kept the utensil on its wings and offered to the king and queen.

They wondered after seeing the boon and in return the queen Zephyranth gave a unique golden fish to Junnu. It was a unique boon with a function of telling the truth. It recognizes the liar but it can be used only once. So it ought to be used in a crucial time.

"Thank you my lady." said Junnu with gratitude.

Daisy, Pansy, Daffodil, Enchanters, Night shade, Marigold, Gilili flower, Belly flower, Chrysanthemum, Day lilies, Night lilies, Roses all together arranged a grand farewell.

Junnu left for her native land with her friend Steffi.

5
DIBLI—DIBLI RETURNS

Kasturi Vijayam|32

When Steffi was out of her land, her son Bruno went out for recreation. After that, its disposition had changed. It could not recognise anyone. Steffi wanted to ascertain other courtiers. But to its astonishment everyone behaved apathetically.

No one was ready to give the correct information including the minister. Steffi wept bitterly. Junnu, Steffi and Ballsy had become strangers to the people of Junnuland.

Junnu took the magic wand and left alone to the forest.

"Warm greetings to you master."

Sage Ananda opened his eyes slowly. "May God bless you my dear. How are you?" "Master, I am in trouble. My people are in miserable condition."

"What happened?" asked Ananda.

Junnu told everything.

Sage Ananda closed his eyes. Junnu eagerly

waited for his words.

"A monster named Dibli-Dibli came to your land in your absence and mesmerised all your people by giving some savouries to your people. So they sated with the pudding available in your land. They don"t obey your orders."

"My God!! How can I help this situation master?"

"Don't worry once give me your magic wand." Ananda turned the wand upside down and applied some herbal paste by chanting a hymn.

"Now take this with you. It provides the savouries you need, along with the pudding."

"Thank you master. But... but... How can I get rid off the monster?"

"You experience a difficult situation then you shall have to depend on your intelligence you will succeed in that and also you can end the life of monster with this wand."

"I am so much grateful to you sir. Now shall I leave master?" "All the best, my blessings will be with you dear."

***

Junnu disguised herself as a villager, directly she went to the market place. It was a place of sundry things. In the heart of the market there was a big tent. A vendor with varieties of savouries was sitting, he was so very busy with the customers.

Junnu pushed them and invaded the interior of the array with great difficulty. "Yes madam, What do you want?"

"Nothing. I came here just to see what was happening. An array of folk is being seen only in your shop, so with great curiosity I came here."

"That's fine. Why cannot you buy some items of snacks in my stall?" "Why not! Sure. Can I taste it before buying?"

"Sure....Have it."

Junnu feigned as really tasted and said "Wow... Delicious! Let me purchase the entire stall."

"M....M....Ma'am!"

"Yeah. Don't worry. I am a landlady. By seeing my attire you might have thought I am a pauper. I need some more. Can you bring tomorrow?"

"Ye...Ye...Ye...Yes... Ma'am. But I can come only for the night market."

"Night market! Why?

"Now a days, these people have changed their life style. Day time they do night work and night time they do day work."

"Oh God! What's the reason for this drastic change?"

"Hey Ma'am! Once you taste these savouries

and see the change in you. Ha …ha," one of the passers-by commented.

"Oh! that's good. Tomorrow, you come with huge stuff because I want to take this as a gift to our dame."

"Your dame….! Who?" "Our princess, Junnu!"

"Oh… I am so fortunate to send this to your princess." "Thank you, see you tomorrow at the same time."

***

The next evening a messenger came to the stall and said "Our princess wants to see you. She liked your savouries."

"Thank you," he said and followed the messenger.

"Greetings! your Highness" Dibli.. Dibli, as the shopkeeper bowed his head.

"Look Mr…. my people are very much fascinated by your tastes, of course me too. They seemed to be sated with our traditional recipes, so we decided to know the secret of your preparation."

"I am honoured Ma'am. I reveal the recipe but on one condition." "Condition? Or Remuneration?"

"Whatever you call, I need the producer of your traditional pudding." "What? Producer! Do you mean to have my magic wand?"

"Yes, of course."

Junnu turned towards the courtiers, they nodded their heads to "give". "But this is our livelihood. How can we lose it?" Steffi mumbled.

"When my people need it heartfully, I should respect their request." Junnu said in order to appease the shopkeeper and accepted the public opinion.

"Okay mister, you can have it. But before offering I have to chant one hymn so that it can acclimatise your ownership."

"Okay your highness, Whatever you say I oblige," said the shopkeeper.

"Look mister, Whatever I chant just you repeat," said Junnu and handed over the magic wand to him.

"Joo…Joo…magic wand…
Joo…Joo…magic wand…
Kiss me…. I am your new master….
Kiss… me …. Upside down."

He was very much happy for the eke out of the wand and in a vivacious mood spelt the words. Immediately the wand turned and the down portion which was coated with the herbal paste turned up, released layers of spicy chilli paste.

He had become blind, shouted in agony and his real form came out. He ran around the court hall haplessly. All the members assembled there and were stunned after seeing the monster.

They adulated their princess Junnu and applauded her ruling.

6
JUNNU'S VERDICT

JUNNU's ADEVENTURES

One snug morning, Junnu was sitting on the lawn. She was in her formals. It was a pink coloured taffeta gown with wavy frills. Her short blonde hair was moving like froth on the water currents.

Her minister who was her cousin approached her for a casual talk. When they engrossed in it, the bell for justice rang near the threshold of the fort.

Junnu told the minister to find out who was in trouble. He informed that two men were waiting for justice. Those men were summoned into the court. Junnu asked the reason for the dispute.

"Your Highness, warm greetings from us. I am Day and he is Night. I am the owner of two acres land.

But he is telling that, the land belongs to him. He is lying.

"No Ma'am, I am the truthful person. You can

enquire about me in my village. I am honest. I beg you to do justice to me."

All the courtiers stared at both of them. Both of them were looking innocent. They could not make out whose version was true. It was a time for lunch. Junnu ordered to serve lunch for both of them along with her. All were surprised. No one understood the intention of the princess. They whispered among themselves. The court was Adjourned. The trial was postponed to the next day.

The following morning, both Day and Night came to court. All the members were eagerly waiting for the verdict. Everyone was tensed. Junnu asked both of them a question.

"How was yesterday's lunch?"

Night replied, "It was so delicious, Your Highness! We are very fortunate to have a royal lunch with you. I felt very happy. I am so grateful to you."

Day said, "Sorry Ma'am, I could not concentrate on the taste of the food. I was very much worried about my property."

Junnu said, "What! You couldn't focus on the taste of gourmet food! You are talking too much."

"Yes, Yes," courtiers whispered.

Day replied "I am sorry mam"

It is okay I can't make out who is the right owner to the fixed asset. Even my minister is also helpless.

So we have decided to put forth two options in front of you.

One is equal distribution of the property to both of you. Second is to transfer the entire property to the upliftment of the poor.

Night said, "I go with the first option Ma'am, that is sharing of property equally between us."

Day objected his proposal. He said, "No Mam, I disapprove this. If you trust me give the entire property to me, or handover the property to the poor."

Junnu was silent for some time and said, "This night deserves for the punishment of the imprisonment of five years. The real owner of this property is Day.

Day's eyes became bright. He bowed his head and said, "Thanks a lot Ma'am. May God bless you."

Night admitted his mistake and begged for pardon.

Junnu said, "You will be forgiven but you should not repeat it in future." "Definitely, thank you madam."

"Ma'am, May we know how did you recognise the culprit?" Bruno asked.

As Day is the real owner, he did not bother

about his food and sleep. By seeing his sunken eyes, we can understand that last night he didn't get sleep.

Secondly, he was ready to leave his property to the poor but not to the greedy person, Night. "But Night expected half of the property because that it would be a free offer to him."

All praised Junnu's intelligence.

***

The neighbour king who was in disguise witnessed the intelligence of princess Junnu. He revealed his identity in the midst of a big applause and honoured her with a powered „Ruby bracelet."

7
MAGIC PILLOW

JUNNU's ADEVENTURES

The king of Ruby land was on a sortie. He came to Junnuland with the queen, the princess and some courtiers. Junnu got the information that a king's camp was held near the outskirts of her land and longing to meet the princess Junnu to develop an amicable rapport between the two kingdoms.

The minister along with some courtiers went personally and received the king and his family.

Junnu revered the king's family and grand arrangements were made to the guests.

After finishing their ablutions Junnu observed that the princess of Ruby land had some abnormality hidden in her beauty. She expressed her doubt. The queen sobbed.

Then the king expressed his woe and told that the princess got shock mentally and lost her memory. Junnu heard it and consoled the couple. She promised that the Ruby princess would be cured soon.

Junnu told them to respite.

Steffi brought the message that polar bear's family visited Junnu land. The adjacent palace was allotted to them.

A soiree was arranged. The guests, Polly and its family, Ruby king and his family attended.

Junnu with her minister and her companions were present there.

"Greetings! your Highness. We are very much thankful to your hospitality and the concern you showed towards our child Polly. Madam a small gift from our side to you, just a token of memory."

Polly's father offered an icy fruit to Junnu and said, "Madam, it gives sweet, aromatic, edible, snow whenever you want. It will be like a smooth creamy butter. A bountiful of it you can have whenever you desire.

"Thank you sire," said Junnu.

"Extremely sorry for my aeon madam. It's a matter of fact, one of my siblings was confined to bed. So I could not come to you immediately."

"No problem dear. By the way, how is your sibling now?" "Now she is healthy and hale."

"Good. Enjoy yourselves with our native recipes," Junnu said and turned towards the Ruby king. "Hope you are satisfied with our customary arrangements."

"Yes madam, thank you very much for your courtesies. If you don't mind here is a small gift from our side."

Junnu smiled and said "What is there to mind? We should maintain harmonious relations between us."

"That's true madam. This is a magic pillow. It sings lullabies. Before it arrants the first lullaby the people around you will sleep. Before it completes the second lullaby the person who lies down on it will be in sound sleep"

"If one will not get sleep?" Steffi enquired.

"There is no question of it till now, the pillow made no such occasion," replied the queen.

The princess was quiet with vague looks.

"Okay let me try once," said Junnu and held the pillow.

It was in azure colour with pinkish bounded lace, it was very soft and cushioned. At the centre of it a tiny pearl button was stitched. The entire surface was studded with rubies. It was a sumptuous article.

Junnu kept it below her head and pressed the pearl button with her right thumb. As soon as she did it the pillow started singing the melodious lullaby. It was like a bundle of magnetic waves passing the musical notes.

Before the completion of the first lullaby everyone in the party involuntarily fell asleep. Junnu awakened alone. Slowly she began yawning. She wanted to control herself from sleeping. Her brain worked smart and she took the magic wand in her hand.

The second lullaby was over. Junnu did not

close her eyes. To her astonishment a handsome young prince appeared in front of her.

Junnu asked "Hey! Who are you?"

The prince gestured that he could not speak.

But Junnu interpreted his gestures in a wrong way that he was hungry. So she offered the ice fruit, in her hand. When she pressed the fruit in between her palms. The sweet fragranced snow fell on his lips.

The prince smiled and started telling his story "Ma'am, before telling about my curse, I must find out. Do you marry me?"

"Marry? No..sorry. I cannot marry you. No doubt you are good looking, handsome guy. But my heart is not ready to accept you as my heart throb!"

"Thank you very much madam. All my worries will end from this moment onwards. The first condition of my release from curse has been fulfilled when you refused my proposal. If you had accepted my proposal, I would have become pillow again. Thank God! I'm saved."

"Yours is a very interesting story. Tell me" Junnu relaxed and sat.

"Madam, I loved this Ruby princess. I am the prince of pearl kingdom. But Farrago, an icy monster changed me like a pillow as he wanted to marry the princess. Ruby king's spies snatched the pillow, that"s me. And handed over to the king. After knowing this the princess shocked and lost her memory.

The Ruby King met a sage. He told the remedy to my curse. According to him, I would be transformed to my original form when the person who lies on the pillow shouldn't get sleep until the second lullaby finishes.

Secondly, sweet smelt delicious snow has to fall on me. Then I can speak out. The third condition is that the lass should reject my proposal.

All the three conditions are satisfied with your kindness. I am indebt of your help."

"Thank God! You are alive and your love is true. So you are free from your curse, now wake up these people," said Junnu.

He closed his eye and chanted a hymn silently. All the members opened their eyes as if they woke up from a dream. All of them surprised after seeing a handsome guy in front of them. The Ruby king flabbergasted. He could not believe his eyes.

Junnu kept miraculous elixir "Didhiya" flower on the forehead of the Ruby princess. She was unconscious after inhaling the scented smell. After few seconds, she woke up and became normal. She recognized her parents and the prince.

The king, in gratitude thanked Junnu.

All were happy. The guests took leave from Junnu and all.

Thereafter, Junnu continued to rule the Junnuland with her benevolence and intelligence.

8
VANISHED WAND

A messenger came from Zucchini land. "He was with an invitation. The king of Zucchini kingdom invited Junnu for a pleasure trip. It also contained that there were some problems in their land and they need to solve the drought with her help.

The minister suspected that something would go wrong. But Junnu was cool and assured the minister that nothing would happen to her, the minister advised the princess to be cautious.

Steffi, Bruno, and some close friends of Junnu set off their journey towards Zucchini land.

***

"Hearty welcome to you Ma'am" the Zucchini king personally received princess Junnu.

"Sorry for the inconvenience, thanks a lot for accepting our invitation".

That evening the Zucchini king discussed their problems with Junnu.

The king described that once the Zucchini land was famous for "long, thin vegetables with a dark green skin."

"In yore days our people were very happy with the crops. Now all the fertile lands had become barren, I am in helpless condition." Said the king.

"By the way what is the reason for this drastic change?" Junnu asked. "It's because of fish rains Ma'am."

"What! fish rains?"

"Yeah, we get number of fishes in the rains."

"Oh, then what is the problem? You get easily the fish and also the ponds full of water. But fish rain quite interesting." Junnu said.

The king told "As you said the fish rains are beneficient but unfortunately a monster flares up these fish rains into flames, they make the crops into ash."

"Do you get frequently these tornados?"

Junnu ascertained. "Of course"

"Don't worry, I will solve your problem." Junnu took her magic wand and made transparent platforms on all the fields. They were high in the sky. The king amazed.

The very evening weather had changed, there was a heavy down pour, all the fish were trapped in the nets above the transparent platforms and the people left the fishes in the ponds.

"Thanks a lot your Highness, we are facing one more obstacle. Please show a remedy for that."

"Yes, What's that?" Junnu asked.

"These are recently formed barren lands. We cannot sow seeds, all the unfavourable conditions influence the sapling growth. Please show us a way." The king requested.

Junnu pondered for sometime. Suddenly an idea dawned on her that the ruby bracelet had the feature of changing any futile thing into a fruitful one.

"Okay let me have a fistful of seeds." Junnu said.

Then she wore the "Ruby bracelet," sowed the seeds and said,"You wait for three days, the fields will be green they never be dried."

"Your Highness you saved our lives. Thank you very much." The king told.

The queen requested, "Dear Ma"am kindly stay with us for a week, we will be happy" Junnu accepted.

***

The monster "Krakatova" came to know that the fields were protected by transparent platforms and the barren lands were going to be changed into fertile lands. He yearned the magic wand and ruby bracelet from Junnu.

He enquired about the companions of the princess.

The monster disguised himself as Bruno and locked the real Bruno in a corner room.

He went inside with Steffi. He fetched both the Bracelet and Magic wand, tactfully he flew far off island.

The very next morning, Junnu came to know that both the magic things, were taken by the monster.

The king felt sad and apologised Junnu. She became blank for some time then decided to meet the sage Ananda.

Junnu rode the horse. Steffi also accompanied her. Rest all returned Junnu Land.

Sage Ananda told, "I can help you to go there. But there you have to depend on your spontaneity.

Take these sacred florets. But you need to utilise this only for one break journey. Also I bless you that a prince will help you. But he is your enemy."

"Enemy! Helps me? How ?" Junnu stunned.

Then they set off to the island. On the way, they stayed for a night in a hamlet. The inn owner had a cock. After their supper, Junnu and Steffi were talking about their journey. The cock went to them.

"Hi guests, I am Kokai. I have come from the island where you have to go now." "How do you know all this ?" asked Junnu.

"Once I was a lad. The monster "Krakatova" came to our village and performed some magic on the road side. I followed him to learn all the magic. Afterwards, I understood that he was a monster. He took me to his island and made me as his slave. Being a smart boy, I learnt all the magic and hymns very soon.

The monster knew that I learnt everything then he made me as his cock.

One day, the monster was sleeping then a bullock-cart with a flock of fowls was going that way to a market place. Cleverly, I fled from there and joined the flock. Then Krakatova woke up with the crescendo made by all the fowls together

------- crock….crock…..crock….----------

He couldn't identify which was his fowl because I disguised myself as a white cock like the other fowls.

The hymns that I learnt from the monster helped me. This inn owner bought me from the market and I told him everything."

"My God! How can you get back your real form?" Junnu asked.

"I know the hymn but a magic feather is needed that is present on the monster's head".

"Oh God! What to do now?" Junnu said.

"Ma'am one thing we do, first let us go to the island. As kokai is acquainted with that area, he can help us." steffi said.

"Yeah, that's good." Junnu said.

The very next morning, they took leave from the inn owner. Junnu used the sacred florets for the horse to fly. They left for the fruit island.

9
ADVENTURES OF JUNNU IN FRUIT LAND- I

JUNNU's ADEVENTURES

Fruit Island was famous for its different kind of fruits irrespective of soil type or climatic conditions.

Its unique fruit is "Golden Pomengo", a hybrid of Mango and Pomegranate. It would be with yellow pulp imbibed with red seeds. If one tasted the fruit one could be changed into desired form.

The orchard was an annexure to the monster "Krakatova's" palace.

Junnu, Steffi and kokai landed near the pineapple plantation. When they alighted, a parrot near the foyer cried "Alert! Alert! Strangers... Strangers."

The cock chanted a hymn. Then the parrot shouted, "Fun...fun...No Strangers.. No strangers. These are our friends. Our trees...Our fruits... Fun.. Fun..."

Foolish parrot shut your mouth. Our master "Krakatova" is livid about your behaviour. I make you permanently dumb. You become mute now."

The dwarf monster sprinkled some seeds on it.

Kokai collected the seeds under its feathers when the dwarf monster left, they came out from a bush.

To enter into the fort they had to cross a moat. Kokai showed them a way from backside of the fort.

When they went the other side, the water in the moat moved swiftly, twisted and finally shaped into a human-being. All the waters jumped out like a man and wanted to catch Junnu.

Kokai got alert and took out a climber with its beak and chanted

" Croak…Croak…Crocky…Crocky…

if you are good just cool down. If not you will be caught in this climber knot and drowned in the green ditch."

The water ebbed. Kokai took out the seeds hidden in its feathers and made into a paste. It sprinkled the paste into waters of moat.

The moat started talking. "Thank you, you gave me voice. I am the prince of Vegan Land. I am Tofu. This monster captured me when I slept in my palace.

"Your Highness, What was the reason behind your capture? If you share I can have a vantage point and can help you to release from here."

"Ha..ha..huh…huh….after all you are a tiny fowl. A trivial creature. How can you help me? I am a prince even then I daunt of my situation."

"Of course as a matter of fact I am not a cock. I am a human being like you but cursed by this monster."

"Oh.. my goodness, please help me." Requested Tofu.

"Definitely, but before that I must know the reason behind your incarceration."

"Yeah, I have three distinctive things with me. One is a satchel that never empties. Whenever you open you get bread, cakes, cookies, chocolates etc all made of vegetable stuff. Second thing a pitcher which is always chock-full, it produces nut milk, the third one is an umbrella, whenever you use this you can go where ever you want.

The monster came to my palace to grab these three but I did not allow and fought. All these three things will work only with my voice vibrations. He has a voice box, he tried to capture my voice but I refused. So he annoyed and changed me into this water body."

"To get your original bodies we must have to chant a mantra and to get mine we have to get the feather from his cap" said kokai.

"Okay, for that we can take the help of my friend the crocodile Alliga- Aligar." said Tofu

"She will be in water. How does she help us?" asked Junnu

"Daily "Krakatova" will come to feed it. When he comes and push my water currents with force Alliga- Aligar traps his hand between its jaws then there is a possibility of falling off the feather." explained Tofu.

"But it will be a risk, if the feather does not fall. Our trial will be futile and Krakatova kills your partner and you on the spot." doubted Kokai.

"No need to perturb. If such situation occurs we take out the feather and push him into the moat." said Junnu.

"May I know who are you?" asked the Vegan land prince

"I am the princess of Junnuland." Junnu said

"So you the princess, I don't want any favour from you, you are our foe." "Foe! Why do you feel so?""

"We are Vegans. We are pure vegetarians but you people feed on animal products. We not even consume curd."

"But it is not the time to bicker." said Junnu.

"Okay it's alright, why did you come here?" Tofu asked "Krakatova snatched our magical items."

"So what, after all for non-living things why did you take risk?"

"It"s not the question of bits and pieces, if those are there in the hands of a malicious person those things will be misused like weapons."said Junnu

"Yes, that's true. Let's wait for tomorrow but where do you hide?" asked Tofu "There is a cavern in this vicinity. Tonight we sleep there." said Kokai

The very next morning dwarf monster came to feed the crocodile.

The crocodile asked "What happened to our mega monster? Why did he not turn up this morning?"

"I know you are fond of him; he went to Himalayas." said the dwarf monster.

"Oh, may I know why?"

"I will tell you, because I trust you. He went there to procure some herbs. If he mixes the juice of herbs with the green apple pulp of our plantation and guzzle it he becomes immortal."

"Oh, that"s fine we would be lucky to have an everlasting king, thank you." "Don"t disclose it to anyone."

"I promise you, I don't reveal. But when he returns?" "He comes back day after tomorrow."

The dwarf monster left the place.

After knowing this Junnu and Tofu decided to stop the monster from becoming immortal.

10
ADVENTURES OF JUNNU IN FRUIT LAND -II

Kokai took Junnu and Steffi to the Pomengo coppice. On the way it showed Junnu the trees, the pillars of the fort, some birds, some statues, some rocks and some hillocks. Kokai said that those were the changed human beings, among them, some were soldiers, some were great warriors and many of them were lay men and women.

The crocodile in the moat was the daughter of a rich merchant; the monster loved that girl so he disguised himself as a young, handsome guy to surmount the heart of the girl. She loved him and walked off with him.

One night she happened to see Krakatova"s real ugly form and fainted, after getting consciousness she vomited on his face. The monster was so irate that he made her into a dreadful crocodile and captivated her in the moat. Kokai told the crocodile Alliga- Aligar to pretend in front of him as still she loved him. So that she could come out with tactics into her real form.

"So if we know the hymn to transform all his enemies into their real forms we can flee from here with ease." said Junnu.

"Yeah, that"s right but.. " said Kokai.

"Why…. But!... Don't you know the hymn?" asked Junnu.

"I don't know the last word of it, because the monster used to chant the last word silently."

"Oh, can we enter into the fort?" asked Junnu.

"Sure. But we cannot enter in our real forms because there will be a mirror in the lobby. Krakatova, the monster can see the people who enter into his palace so we will be caught." said kokai, the cock.

"Then how can we enter into it?" Steffi asked

"We can change our forms by eating those pomengoes still there is a problem in that. Once we get the desired form we can get back the real forms by getting sprinkled the waters of moat. But when we change ourselves into the new form we forget about the remedy." said Kokai.

"Nothing to worry. All of us need not change at a time; first we change Steffi into a dwarf monster. After its regaining its original form, you change." Junnu said.

"Sorry ma'am I cannot be changed, the monster changed me with the feather on his cap. We have to get the feather." said Kokai.

"Okay ma'am first let me eat the Pomengo to change into the dwarf monster, once I change I go into the palace and search for the magical items. If the monster sees in mirror he thinks I am his loyal dwarf monster." said Steffi.

It was late mid-night the tall security monsters were in sound sleep. The water in the moat became still, it formed like a crystalline platform and they walked over that and entered into the fort.

Steffi ate that fruit and changed herself into the dwarf monster. Junnu and Kokai waited outside the palace. Steffi entered alone. Its image was caught in mirror, it was seen by Krakatova who was in Himalayas but he did not suspect.

Steffi walked towards the north corner in the central hall where the image would not be caught. There was a vase in the corner unknowingly Steffi touched it, at once it went interior into the ground. The core of the earth was dark it fell down unconscious.

Junnu's sixth sense told something went wrong inside. Without any secondary notion Junnu jumped inside. Her image was caught by the magic mirror. Krakatova saw Junnu and smelt the peril, without further ado, he set off.

Junnu understood the hazard. She understood the intimidated situation. Involuntarily she broke the mirror with vase in the corner; underneath there was a vent where she fell. She kicked Steffi. It got consciousness and started barking in agony.

"Hey Steffi what happened?" asked Junnu.

"Nothing. But we cannot see anything, it's dark here, we can grope some hard substances." said

Steffi.

"Of course. Now there is no ample time, the monster knew that we are here so he could arrive at any time. Before that we must evacuate this area." said Junnu.

While telling this Junnu's hand fell on a heap. A cloth was unfolded, below that there was a heap of diamonds, bright shimmering rays came from it, they could see all the magical items. Steffi gathered all and dumped in a copper container, both of them came out.

They saw all the broken pieces of mirror joined together, everything could be visible to the monster. Junnu wanted to prevent the unification of the broken pieces, but she was helpless. The magic wand turned towards the window, through the window Junnu saw a sand hill, an idea struck to her, she ordered the magic wand to bring some sand, meanwhile she broke the mirror again, Junnu chanted a hymn….

"Joo..Joo…Magic wand….

Joo…Joo..Magic wand…..

Jo..Jo.. Join not….

Joo… Jaa…. Magic wand.."

And sprinkled the sand on the broken pieces

of mirror to prevent joining of the glass pieces.

Junnu and Steffi met Kokai outside. All the three went to the moat. Kokai sprinkled some water on Steffi and chanted a mantra. It got back its original form as a German shepherd dog.

"Dear wand, how can the moat and all get their body shapes?" asked Junnu.

The wand moved towards the copper container, Steffi took out all the magical items one after the other, finally a small, multicoloured, antique box was taken out. The wand bent towards it, Junnu understood that it had some power.

Kokai came near to it and said, "Yes, it is the voice box it might have the „silent word" let me try, at any time the monster may come here." Kokai said and started chanting…

" Shrooooo… Broooo….Croak…

Hroooom…Drooom…Croak…

Poi… Goi….Thoi….Coi…..Coi….." and stopped.

Kokai did not know the last word of the mantra, and then the voice box repeated..

"Shroooo…Broooo…Croak…

Hroooom…Drooom…Croak…

Poi…Goi…Thoi…Coi…Coi…

Gu… Gu… Guguva….."

Kokai chanted the last word silently. The entire moat was emptied, the crocodile turned up into a beautiful lass, the moat waters changed into Vegan prince. All the aquatic animals turned into different animals, birds, men and women. Some of them were princes, princesses rest were all the lay men and women.

Among the animals some were trained, some were tamed, some were wild. Junnu controlled all with her magic wand. Kokai was the only creature which could not get back its original body, it eagerly awaited the monster.

Junnu fought with monster"s army by using her magic wand. All of them fell unconscious, the princes and princesses took their horses, wild animals went into the nearby forests under the guidance of Junnu with magic wand, she invited all the people to her land. They had thanked her and left.

Kokai was dull. Junnu consoled him, Vegan prince waited for the monster near the green apple wood. The pomengo tree was uprooted and smashed, the monster came and understood the earnest situation. He perplexed.

After seeing the Vegan prince he understood that someone who acquainted with his island accompanied him. Vegan prince Tofu directly attacked with his sword, the monster was about to chant a mantra. Junnu climbed with her magic wand on his head and took out the feather from his cap.

Kokai was smeared by the feather. In no time the cock turned into a lad. He was active and energetic. He bowed his head at the feet of Junnu, but the monster ambushed Junnu from behind, the wand fell down, Junnu's hair was in the hands of Krakatova. Steffi held the wand between its jaws.

The ferocious Vegan prince killed the monster. He opened his umbrella and made Junnu to sit on his horse behind him.

After the death of the monster the entire island burnt into ashes. The umbrella flew towards Junnu's land. Steffi and Kokai followed them with all magical items.

Junnu took out the magic fish and found out if the Vegan prince was good because Guru Ananda cautioned her that her enemy would help her. The golden fish said that the foe had become friend with good nature.

The golden fish could be used only once so Junnu utilised that to choose her spouse.

It was sumptuous party arranged by Junnu's minister, the ice cream made with nut milk, vegan cakes, cookies, dates, pudding, varieties of savouries served in surplus.

With great pomp and pompadour the princess of Junnu land „Junnu" had wedlock with the prince „Tofu" of Vegan land. Thereafter they lived happily with Steffi, Bruno, Kokai and all.

SUPPORTS

- **PUBLISH YOUR BOOK AS YOUR OWN PUBLISHER.**

- **PAPERBACK & E-BOOK SELF-PUBLISHING**

- **SUPPORT PRINT ON-DEMAND.**

- **YOUR PRINTED BOOKS AVAILABLE AROUND THE WORLD.**

- **EASY TO MANAGE YOUR BOOK'S LOGISTICS AND TRACK YOUR REPORTING.**

www.ingramcontent.com/pod-product-compliance
Lightning Source LLC
LaVergne TN
LVHW012125070526
838202LV00056B/5867